AF437542

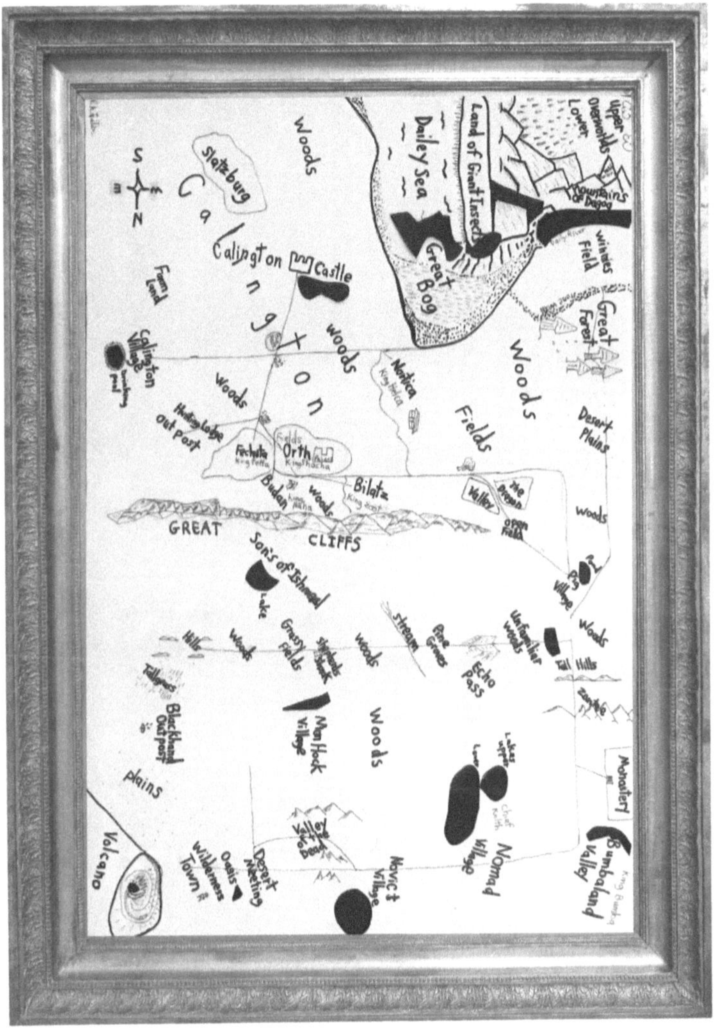

S
W E
N
Upper
Overworlds
Lower
Land of Great Insect
Mountains of Bagog
Slatzburg
Woods
Dailey Sea
Great Bog
Winkies Field
Calington
Castle
Farm Land
Canyon
Woods
Great Forest
Calington Village
Woods
Nortica
Woods
Fields
Desert Plains
Hostrog Lodge Outpost
Fields
Orth
Fatlata
Budah
Bilatz
Valley
The Broom
Open Field
Woods
GREAT
CLIFFS
Village
Sons of Ishmael
Lake
Woods
Unfamiliar Woods
Tall Hills
Woods
Hills
Woods
Grassy Fields
Stream
Bone Groves
Echo Pass
Village
Blackhand Outpost
Marffick Village
Woods
Monastery
plains
Valley of the Dead
Desert Meeting
Oasis
Wilderness Town
Upper
Lower
Nomad Village
Bumbaland Valley
Volcano
Navic't Village

Calington Castle VIII

The Monsignor's Notes
On
"The Tree Of Life"
&
Other Meditations
(Includes)
Breaking Addictions

R. A. Feller

ISBN 979-8-9894920-1-5 (paperback)
ISBN 979-8-9894920-0-8 (eBook)

Printed in the United States of America

$\mathcal{A}$s the Monsignor at the Monastery of Ostrog, I have given R. A. Feller, friend to those at Calington Court, liberty to take my notes and write them into meditations for clarities sake.

We met in secret throughout many a night and his pen seemed to reflect my thoughts. Speaking to him of all of my adventures, quite vigorously at times, we talked 'til having a like-mindedness to pass on my wealth of a heritage of wisdom.

My teachings are a culmination of over forty years of study, which I saw him apply to his life. Now that his knowledge has become wise, he walks in the light. A very sobering *Feller* to talk with to say the least as when challenged he prays 'til God makes things right. I've watched Him move on him every time.

My responsibilities of managing the monastery and the affairs of life have hindered me in my studies, but not the same story for the author of my notes who I watched pen diligently night and day while looking into the light of God, with a sort of envy and yet even sorrow at times.

Talking to him, I saw that he had something new to share each time as I watched him grow in his relationship with The Great One during our encounters each year.

Now he is a man of substance as his life has abundantly been filled, seasoned as wise as a serpent and as harmless as dove. He takes patient time to be gentle and listen with love. I have watched him enjoy the presence of the Lord where turning matters over to Him strife he avoids. For he has kept his hand in God's 'til becoming a reward. Now here is his writing that I know you'll enjoy.

The Tree of Life

In my over forty years of studying full reality through the given laws of divine nature, I have drawn conclusions that are in this book. Every tree has the essence of a God given nature. This meditation will discuss what God has to say about all the design of His creation.

Pause and ponder each step of coming into being:

Void

Blood of Christ

Silence

Elements

Alone

Darkness

Time

Awareness

Emotion

Expression

Word

Vibration

Harmony

Motion

Friction

Heat

Fire

Light

Vision

Glory

Brilliance

Embrace

Love

Truth

Sound

Balance

Formation

Spirit

Creation

Firmament

Sky

Night

Morning

Wind

Water

Land

Rain

Paradise

Season

Soil

Seed

Root

Stem

Plant

Animal

Man

"I see men as trees walking" were the words of a blind man being healed by Jesus laying His hands over His eyes.

When God creates, He takes a little piece of the being of Himself and sparks forth life through the light of love in the essence of His omnipresence in everything. This is the glue that holds all of creation together as God as creator expresses Himself.

In the beginning, God created by the use of His expression of word, which generated pure light for the truth of the Spirit of His love to be made manifest.

Now moving on the surface of the face of the waters, which He has formed with creation set in order, God created mankind in His own image; male and female He created them. (It is my feeling that as a threefold cord cannot easily be broken, He did not create a man to birth another humankind by himself or female to reproduce after herself for this could spark an uprising against Himself, should mankind have had equal power. I further suspect that by creating two separate human beings to honor the truth of love, He could have fellowship with them together as one without the threat of an uprising as what happened when Lucifer fell from his pride in rebellion to become Satan here in time. Perhaps God divided their power to be complete as one and have unity to further create by the truth of His light of love. I further believe this truth is spiritually conveyed in the creation of hermaphrodites, which appear periodically unto this day.)

So, God blessed Adam by giving him dominion over the whole of all creation, plants, animals, fish, and birds alike, telling them to be fruitful and multiply. Nothing good was withheld from them in God's justice. However, there was the fruit of the knowledge of good and evil, pleasing to the eye with a wonderful fragrance that happened to smell very sweet, but when the fallen angel, Satan, suggested, "You certainly will not die but become wise from its fruit. Eat of it and you will become like God," to man's helpmate, Eve. Adam was by her side. The fruit was incomplete at its core with decay and death, for God had warned Adam that the day he would eat of it he would surely die. Taking on its incomplete nature, he lacks the substance of His own complete image as he listened to Satan's lust in place of God.

The First man failed to heed the voice of love, which was proof that he no longer reflected the true image of God's embrace. Adam now spoke from darkness rather than light where his now sin nature is missing the presence of God.

All men are now trapped in the length of the breadth within the heights and the depths of time, cut off from God's presence by the heritage of Adam's bloodline of death. Severed from the vine of life; we now die.

Mankind is a branch cut from the vine of life in the dark and because of this, there is decay and death. Without brilliant light, minds go dim and by making poor choices, we hurt ourselves while in the confusion of the dark. Why else would we become like a bull in God's delicate world and trample it underfoot?

Yet, the most intelligent question remains deceptively hidden from our sight, "How do we reconnect to the vine which produces life without losing our living souls by returning to the dust of this Hellish fallen world we find ourselves in?"

After realizing I have been grafted into death by being an offspring to Adam, I knew I lacked wisdom on how to escape it. Although I searched, I could not find a way out as I watched men die. For man ate of the fruit of the knowledge of good and evil which severed him from being bonded to drawing from the life of God. Corruption entered his living blood and he became incomplete by complete rebellion by a betrayal against God.

Facing the dilemma of being grafted into the vine of death, I do not desire to dry out on a broken branch that dies.

Now by the mercy and grace of God, He has given me vision to see that unless I am grafted back onto the tree of life before leaving my body here on earth, my living soul will be perpetually drained at the end of my days. I have a living soul which is in a degenerative state of perpetual death, fashioned in a corruptible form while my body dies if eternal life is missed.

My soul, a seed of energy, would no longer be my own to enjoy in an earthen vessel nor translated over into eternity to be completely reunited to God to further enjoy the resurrection of heaven. Beware, demons drain all who do not know God at the end of their life as they instead become planted here on earth to become a dragon's prize.

God resolved this dilemma with the wisdom of the Trinity by the Holy Spirit and His Son, which generated a force of energy to burn us off the branch of sin. There is now a new graft of a bond in love, knit so tight, that its intensity generates the essence of a pure light from the truth of it. God foreknew that He was to send His Son even before the foundation of the earth was laid by His blood.

Although the bond of the relationship with His Son was highly valued by love, The Father was willing to lay it down to reconcile with Adam's offspring which are created to further His love. John 3:16-17 "For God so loved the world that He gave His only begotten son that none should perish. For God did not send His Son into the world to condemn it, but that all have everlasting life with Him."

Now just as one vine caused death to enter in by the fruit of knowledge of good and evil from the realm of paradise unto this fallen earth, another vine as "The Tree of Life" is here as well as there in a parallel realm that that gets intersected by a ray to bring us back, reconnecting us to God's universe. This is why that little fruit of the Holy Eucharist containing the flesh and blood of Jesus Christ is such a necessity, for it translates us out of the darkness of mystery. Thy kingdom come, thy will be done on earth as it is in heaven. We are being translated out from this world and into heaven as we are now receiving our glorified bodies in heaven while on earth.

God's seed of love was planted by His Holy Spirit light. A vine that still stands to restore His relations with mankind till this day if they so choose to be grafted back to eternity by His warmth of love.

Truth and love came back together with a balance of harmony that our focus outside the realm of time would be restored where joined onto His vine again. I do rejoice!

For religion is not an animal pen but a springboard up to understand heaven.

At one time, I tried to have God's power work for me rather than surrender to His will. In my pride, I did not know how to acknowledge my helplessness before Him to get meaning out of life. For when I tried to understand life on my terms, I was foolish and He did not answer. So, I tried other spirits which led me into addictions. A spirit other than God's had me bound up in knots and in a servitude with no escape from my lack of understanding life instead.

Breaking Addictions

The good Lord said, "Be still and know that I am God." Now let us do so, that we can rest from the busyness of the day and focus our minds on the light of God.

God is a God of mercy but if you choose not to go to Him for help in times of trouble or struggle, He cannot help you. For when trying to handle problems on our own without going to Him, we turn God away.

It says in the book of Psalms, "My God is an ever present help in time of need." and "I will lift up my eyes unto the hills from which comes my strength because all my strength comes from the Lord above."

Ask yourselves, "Would someone take the time to write these words if it were a lie?"

A man who became a king wrote these words as a shepherd boy.

David, who slayed the lion, wolf, and bear - who also slew a giant named Goliath in the name of the Lord of Hosts (whose name was to be revealed at a later time), did not handle the giant on his own in pride - a spirit that turns God away from helping. He invited The Lord into battle by calling on Him and not relying on himself.

I repeat, the scriptures say, "My God is an ever present help in time of need."

When we do not agree with God, we call Him a liar and abuse Him by turning Him away like when we crucified Him on the cross. Yet in His mercy, the Lord of Hosts said, "Forgive them father for they know not what they do."

Any addiction is a giant to us but not to a God who is merciful. For when we abuse His property - as we are not our own because we belong to Him - we abuse Him who fashioned our living soul out of the Spirit of the essence of His being as the Psalm says, "We were knit together in our mother's womb (He planted and crafted us by His own hand as we are made of a living soul that dwells within soil), for when I was being made in secret, fashioned in the depth of the earth, You saw me formed." Those who do not acknowledge being crafted by Him, He does not hear except by mercy.

If you call yourself your own, God will not protect you, but if you humble yourself at the throne of your heart and step down and allow Him to reign, thus says the Lord of Hosts our God, "I will only protect you if you humble yourself to my authority.

I need to be the love of your life and you will be the apple of my eye. Let go of greed for great gain and then I will light the torches of your hearts and keep back the darkness of dragons of evil spirits that you do not see. The spirits behind lust for power and pleasure that causes you to have cravings and urges will never be satisfied, for you are in hell in the realm of sheol.

Weep and wail… and if you return to me as your Lord of Hosts, you will be satisfied forever. For when you are helpless, I can be your ever present help in time of need instead of your drug of choice - false gods - which are cruel taskmasters that you unknowingly serve.

Turn from your ways. For I have heard your tears which do not have answers. If you humble yourselves and come to me in the name of my Son whom I sent as the Lord of Hosts, you shall be restored to eternal life and receive your salvation.

I the Lord your God have spoken."

"Remember: When you are powerless, I can be powerful in your life. So, recognize what I have given you, as your life is a part of Me. Stop putting Me to death in abortion and do not turn to false gods to ease the burden of your pains, then you shall live in freedom as my love will restrain and protect you forever."

"Lord, I want to follow You with all that's in my heart until I know you completely. Give me your life and I shall live forever. Amen."

How does one get to know God better to be able to speak to him in freedom so they do not have to be afraid on earth? **The proverbs say, "The Fear of the Lord is the beginning of wisdom. If you acknowledge Him in all your ways then He will direct your path.** When you are at peace, you have vision to enter God's domain and see His goodness. What this means is that cultivating gratitude adds up. For when you can see how **The Lord of Hosts** has blessed you with all He has given you in the little things, then you can become aware of God in all things. This is how we enter His Kingdom to be blessed in everything.

I discovered this when I was cooking break-fast one morning to take away my hunger. It was as though the Lord tapped me on the shoulder as if to say, "How come you are letting your stomach dictate to you without considering me?"

Right then I realized that I needed to thank the Lord. As I did, I became more aware of how He was blessing me and it caused me to enter into His world. Now, I was no longer just preparing a meal cutting vegetables. Now I was preparing a meal that God had blessed me with in each specific detail of prepa-ration. Hands, fingers, and a knife for cutting my red pepper, onions, squash, cheese, and so on, that He had provided for me became a part of the reality of His Kingdom. The more I acknowledged Him in little things, breaths to breathe, a tongue for tasting flavors, ears for hearing, a mouth for speaking, and the framework of a body to house my living soul, the more prevalent He became till I walked through His door to enter more deeply into a relationship with Him.

Yes! God makes us faithful with a little of Himself before much of Himself. As it says in the Psalms, "The deep calls unto the deep." When we know Him more intimately, it makes it easier to call upon Him in the heat of any giant dragon spirit of addiction battle because we are aware that He is with us at all times. Then He becomes our ever present help in time of need. For when we are aware that our Lord walks with us hand in hand, we are in the light of eternity.

There is no place for anything which lurks in darkness to catch us unaware anymore when receiving a love for His truth above all else. Sensing our actions in the presence of God's kingdom to call upon in our midst in full light at will, we can now see when our actions are ungrateful and feel the weight of a bad attitude. This is what prevents us from being dragged away by any addiction.

For now we are receiving eternal life from The God who has a full measure of His love instead, which we are fed by being open to receive it. Next, having the stability of a firm foundation in the Messiah in an unstable world, we're saved as we have a solid platform to build a relationship with a God who will never leave us nor forsake us. His flesh and blood of the new covenant is real food as eternal life now flows through our veins to keep us content. The Spirit which crafts us during this thanksgiving meal co-mingles with and joins us to The God that brings fresh life, which is better than any spirit of beastly addiction or otherwise. I have learned in my over 40-year walk with Jesus Christ that the only thing I cannot be addicted to is the life which comes from Him.

We were dying in our transgressions and trespasses against God; for the wages in the areas of where we are missing the presence of the Father of

Creation within the fiber of our beings is called sin. Yet the gift of God which surpasses all our understandings to comprehend is eternal life and in the here and **now only being alive can satisfy.** This is what Jesus Christ The Lord of Hosts, Messiah, came to bring us. As He is the essence behind His word, which opens the door to the truth of His love that cares for our hearts as they yearn to now engage everyone who can acknowledge they need to be married to Him. Which means do not cheat on Him. For if you fall back into a dark pit, **by choice,** there is no guarantee that you will find the mercy of God's light or the bond of His loves embrace again.

So, be separate. Come out from among the spirits of this world and Touch not the unclean thing. Keep striving to enter in the narrow gate asking God to change you into the likeness of his image of Holiness by calling on God to make you holy. Then He will keep you by the power of His free gift of grace which will allow you to enter into all He has to offer by the door of His Holiness. For it is living in holiness that God can trust you as well as you trust Him to show you around His Kingdom. "For would

you let a liar, a thief, or a destroyer into your house?"
Now for the good news: I was a lost sheep, but by God's mercy He has allowed me as He will you as long as you have breath in sincerity of faith and heart back into His kingdom.

The cycle that needs
to be broken!

Higher power < All else = Prison. No hope - You do not have the power to change your situation. You cannot see your way out of your discomfort - You are just plain stuck to be trapped where you are when your Higher Power is < all else.

Diagrams

$\mathcal{P}$icture 1: We have been set in motion by spirits of the world since birth. /\/\/\/\/\/\/\/\/\ and try different things while searching for stability.

"Be still and know that I am God." /\/\/\/\/\/\/|_|\/\ Stability begins when we are still and firm /\/\| _________ on the firm foundation of God _______ to receive a loving relationship with Him on a foundation of peace. Then joy is produced to become our strength. "The joy of the Lord is our strength."

This is how I came to know this. For at one time, my life was so dark I could not put two thoughts together.

#1 In eternal life there is a free flow of love from God.

#2 Once in the world we suffer abuse from societal and spiritual darkness. Not being able to find love from God, we get hurt and withdraw into a knot and a part of us goes numb while trying to protect ourselves in our prideful wisdom.

#3 The tighter our knots get, they start to seem normal till all goes numb and we deny their existence.

Love becomes blocked and we start to associate pain with love because at least we know it belongs to us. We stop loving others where feeling comfortably numb in our abuses and/or addiction of choice, entering into darkness, we plainly stop seeing our hurts.

Diagram 1

#1 When in motion, we are in an off-balanced darkness and are not in touch with the emotional

boundaries around our centers which leaves us feeling uneasy.

- When we are not aware of our personal space, which is an arms length around us with our hearts at our center, we get abused every time our peace gets disrupted as we have no vision to comprehend love. "A people perish from a lack of vision."

Diagram 2

\|/

/|\

"The simple pass on and get punished," for they do not know they are getting emotionally overrun, bruised, and abused. Emotional bruises are worse than physical ones as they cause our emotions to disconnect from our thoughts and leave us feeling numb as darkness sets in to dim our minds.

We need to be trained to keep our peace by trusting God to remain in the moment or we'll lose ourselves in further darkness.

Diagram 3

After being overrun, I got angry. I pushed back in anger and lost my peace and my ability to love in the process.

Diagram 4

Yes, in my act of prideful wisdom and lack of expression, I raged to keep people away and became like my rebellious abusers. I became addicted to my spirit of anger until becoming consumed by it.

Diagram 5

$$| \; | \; |$$
$$| \; | \cdot | \; |$$
$$| \; | \; |$$

Walls of rage filled anger in my feeble attempt to keep abusers away. I became locked in a prison within myself until all went numb, blank, and dark inside my mind.

Diagram 6

$$\cdots$$
$$\cdots + \cdots$$
$$\cdots$$

Losing sight of my own actions, I also became an abuser without even knowing it.

R. A. Feller

Poem

Twisting and turning,

my heart has a yearning,

while my craving burns within.

There's a thought that urges me on.

Relax, you can be calm.

I'll fix you up.

Another uneasy day, I am your friend.

Be your Help in time of need?

You'll make it through, have another on me.

I notice my aging body, my youth departs.

"Here, I am waiting.

Steady now, relief! Do not forget,"

says the spirit behind the god of cigarettes.

Why deprive yourself, have comfort, enjoy!

The pleasure of my smoke, you cannot ignore.

All voice of reason drowns as the body sags in age.

Sight in end, no light to shine in hazy, crazy eyes.

Cunningly baffled by the dragon drug inside

Soul sucked, till you're coughed out into its
mouth.

In a feelings grid, our emotions and thoughts are cross stitched together evenly in a tight-knit fabric that reflects the glory of God's loving light.

```
E M O T I O N S        The peace of God
T++++++++++++++        which surpasses all
H++++++++++++++        understanding will guard
O++++++++++++++        your heart and minds.
U++++++++++++++
G++++++++++++++
H ++++++++++++++
T++++++++++++++
S++++++++++++++
      FEELINGS
```

```
E M O T I O N S        When stress is not
T+++++++ ++++++++      turned over.
H++++++ ++++++++++     Thoughts and emotions
O++++++ +++++++++      become separated.
U+++++++++ +++++       Depression happens
G+++++ +++++++         here as well.
H ++++++ ++++++++++    "Be not conformed to this
T+++++++ +++++++       world, be transformed
S+++++++++++++++       by the renewing of
      FEELINGS         your minds."
```

```
E M O T I O N S          "Be not conformed to this
T+++++++++++++++         world, be transformed
H++++++++++++++          by the renewing of
O++++++++++++++          your minds."
U++++++++++ +++++
G+++++ +++++++
H +++++ ++++++++++
O++++++ +++++++++
U+++++++++++++++
T++++++++ ++++++++
S+++++++++++++++
FEELINGS
```

Where there are dark spaces within the mind between our thoughts and emotions, our feelings become disturbed. Demon serpents enter here to nest and lay eggs which hatch to eat away the mind with dark fiery thoughts of their own. This is how we get distracted and are deceived into looking from seeing the light of God's love. "Walk in the light while you have the light so that darkness does not overtake you."

Diagram 7

Figures #1 & #2 When we have boundaries of love and truth in a truly balanced way, there is light for protection from all darkness to make the best choices for a full life.

MAD-GLAD-SAD is the full range of all our emotions. If they are out of balance, we are left in the dark and make poor choices and harm ourselves.

Clear vision allows you to see your value in the light of truth. This is where emotions connect with your thoughts to honor the God of eternal life with your feelings for the best choices in life.

With balance, we can sense when unbalanced people want to abuse us. They are unhealthy and need to be prayed for so that God will shine His light of truth to guide them out of darkness or we will abuse ourselves and others when our feelings are off balance and experience harm. For when you have love minus truth, it turns into a self-love which brings confusion. People worship the creature of self to meet their needs rather than meet the needs of their creator, which is to love Him back in an honest way in the freedom of the pattern of truth and all of its laws, nature included.

More Diagrams:

Figure A. When hooked on your drug of choice while off balance in a relationship to a person, place or thing, our visions of God's love becomes unclear and confusion dims the mind.

Figure B. There is freedom in being balanced, centered, and comfortable in your own skin.

Figure C. In a healthy relationship, boundaries are respected and not violated. While balanced in a position of peace, there is serenity. There is vision when you notice where you begin and end as you're able to remain at peace.

Figure D. When feeling safe and at peace, you can open up your boundaries and let others draw closer towards intimacy.

Figure E. There is marriage with God and anyone else who has unity with Him.

Here is something to consider: In the upper room when Jesus was among His disciples, there were four different relationships going on while the twelve were in His presence.

John had his head on Jesus' bosom. Peter and James were approached by the other twelve to ask John who would betray Him and Judas who betrayed The Lord for personal gain.

Finishing Diagram

Higher Power > All else = Freedom for satisfaction. Both gratitude and bonding love are kept in balance when returning affection. What is truly real has a love flow that locks out all addiction when your Higher Power is > All else.

Hearing God's Voice

We all hear the true and living voice of God in varying degrees until we choose not to listen to it any longer. God's truth leads us out of a dark self and into the bosom of a present love. We next start to comprehend His light and love others, which He loves as well. For the essence of His being is in all of us, but not all can receive the truth of this. Yet, for those who can embrace the light and the life of His love, though they be lost in darkness are now found forever, outside of living in the taste of a staleness of death. What is dead produces the foul taste of death, as what is dead produces more death. This is why Jesus said, "Let the dead bury the dead." For He knew that He came to give us eternal life to replace what is dead in the kingdom realm of this fallen world where Satan resides to keep it under his cloak of darkness. Those who have murder in their hearts against anyone is not from the kingdom that belongs to God. He being Creator says, "Love one another." It is only in the essence of His being that all live, even while confused in darkness or otherwise.

Jesus said, "Let he who is without sin, (or self-righteous in judgment), cast the first stone." Anyone who has motive to do harm to anyone else doth not have the love of God in his heart and lies to himself or anyone else as we are all created by God.

God's desire is that none should perish, but all have the gift of eternal life right now with Him, "The kingdom of heaven is from within." This is where change from darkness to light takes place. This is where the world, the flesh, and the devil gets cast out, that we may walk within God's resurrection by translation.

Moses did not see this at first, when he killed an Egyptian to protect one of his own blood kinsman, for he failed to see that the bloodline of his kin was still corrupted and that it would still end in death. It was not until forty years later that Moses would be able to hear and receive God's voice from Christ, Messiah. Jesus said it Himself, "Before Abraham was, I AM." When everything else that came between him and the truth of God's inner embrace of love had been removed from his life, it left room for the full presence of God's light and life to eventually move in. For later on His face had to be veiled from others as the intensity of God's light shown. Yet now at the burning bush experience, Moses was still in a place of enough darkness in the wilderness of this world that He was not fully trusting in God. As he had expressed, he was slow of speech and could not speak to the Egyptians or even his own. So, God encouraged his faith by sending him help by a staff, turning into a serpent as a sign to others and his brother Aron who was given a boldness to speak for Him, until a time he would grow in his relationship with God where he could be judged as living and not spiritually dead.

When you have tried the any of everything in this world and realize that you are in a wilderness of mirages, the fleshly will no longer satisfy the devil's taste of death. Are you ready to acknowledge a world of spirits that drain and block you from receiving the Spirit which brings life? Then look no further than the blood of Christ, for it is alive with what it really has to offer. If you can acknowledge that you're dying and have an eternal soul inside that needs to be transferred into a new glorified and living body, one which can house the freshness of what lives forever. Be ready, for eternal life can ignite and take your soul through heaven's door of Christ while still alive on earth.

Call out to Jesus and ask Him to deliver you from the taste of death and you will have the gift of the messiah, which is life.

The Church

The Church of Christ is the bride through water baptism and she receives her bridegroom at every thanksgiving meal called the Holy Eucharist, which was started by Jesus Christ at the last supper in the offering of Himself as the New Covenant. This is the root of the vine which all scriptures point to in order to rightly divide the word of truth that came to bear witness of this over two hundred years later.

Jesus said, "I am the vine, you are the branches and apart from Me you can do nothing." So, unless we are drawing from the blood of the vine of the New Covenant, you will wrestle scripture to your own destruction in the same way as the jewish leaders called Pharisees did. For these leaders of their nation searched the scriptures believing there was life in them within their essence, but they missed the fact that they pointed to God's Son of the New Covenant, Jesus Christ.

Yes, by simply believing in Jesus as the anointed Messiah, any can become grafted back from being a broken branch from the dead bloodline of Adam. For by the living vine of God by the living blood of Jesus the Christ is where all will find eternal life. This is what sustains to keep all alive throughout the living organism called the church.

I mentioned that the root of the New covenant is the flesh and blood of Jesus as He has said, "Unless you eat of My flesh and drink of My blood, you will have no part with Me."

From here, the vine shoots upward to sustain more lives as those who accept God's plan for eternal life become grafted in as branches, bearing buds of tender green leaf till seed or perhaps a flower which will turn into a seedling of fruit.

Yes, the tree bears leaves as fed by the roots to tell of what manner of seed fell into the ground by its leaf. The leaf is a reflection, a testifier of the rest of the tree. Now, if one just looks at a leaf, they can tell the whole design of where it came from by comparing it to another tree of the same variety or of fruit in the same way. Do not get mixed up, though. For although the leaf or fruit testifies of the tree, it is not the whole tree. The leaf or fruit is only an indicator as a reflection and not the whole truth of the tree but a part of it. So, any who say that the leaves of scripture are the whole tree are mistaken and destined to believe in a lie as once was I. For when the complete truth is not in you, a spirit of religion hides like a serpent in the branches of a tree to devour any fruit of life. "I see men as trees walking" were the words of a blind man being healed by Jesus laying His hands over His eyes until the second time He laid His hands over His eyes to restore fullness of sight. For unless we are firmly planted, rooted, and grounded in love, we lack fullness of life and become like the fig tree without figs outside of Jerusalem which Jesus cursed.

The demons know scriptures and they tremble in their seduction of instruction which leads to destruction. For as dragon spirit winds keep the leaves moving on the tree, they sway the branch till it snaps from its weight of knowledge without wisdom applied by an inner life. Here the branch is completely driven away and kept from discovering its flesh and blood roots where the resurrection allows us to enter back into heaven's shalom present moment with God. Yes, it is missed and a counterfeit salvation is received in deception to replace the fullness of life.

The first time I received the Holy Eucharist with understanding, I tasted something different from the flesh and blood roots of Christ as grace called me back home into eternal life. I am in this world and no longer of it, as now is the kingdom of heaven at hand, for the serpent has been cast out of my tree. Yet, I still believe that God has mercy and is able to meet everyone in each stage of their spiritual growth if they are truly searching for Him with all their hearts.

Heritage

We have no heritage here on earth because you cannot trust in someone who is going to die, but lives. I have seen the hand of God move in many healings and this is how I know that Jesus Christ still lives.

All our thoughts are spiritual and you must realize that there is evil in the world. It comes from a fallen angel, Satan, which tries to cut us off from God's love by bringing division between not only the thoughts within us, but all of mankind. For when we do not have full feelings with emotions and thoughts knit tightly together to reflect God's light, darkness seeps in through the cracks and what it brings with it. There are spirits that hide within cracks of darkness to distract from the reflection of God's pure light.

They divide and bring confusion to a mind to keep it dim within the dark. For with a single mind there is light for us to see that we can enter a full relationship with God and understand His love.

Knowing God is to know eternal life and if you do not have it, you will taste the taste of a repetitious boredom by living in the mundane as you are eating the stale bread of death while disconnected from God's vine of life.

It is imperative that we receive our bloodline of life heritage by way of flesh and blood from the vine of Jesus Christ, or we will not receive eternal life. There will be no guarantee of it unless we follow God's plan to the letter. For, "Broad is the road to destruction and narrow is the road to salvation and there are few that find it." God's plan is not grievous, He only asks you to admit that without His guidance life is impossible to manage. Then ask for Him to change it by trusting on the Blood sacrifice He has provided to satisfy Himself. The sacrifice is that of His Son, for only Jesus Christ has the Blood that lives to satisfy this requirement as by His own perfection in an imperfect world, He reunites everyone to the God of all creation.

All human beings have an eternal soul and the bible says, "The wages of sin are death, but the gift of God is eternal life." If we die and remain grafted into the vine of death here on earth, our living souls of energy will remain planted in this fallen world. We face being harvested by demons in a perpetual state of dissatisfaction which will release energy to feed them, instead of being allowed freedom to continue on with glorified bodies that God has prepared for us.

In physics, I learned that energy is never used up, it is either transferred or stored. Our energy is traded for the use of demons to manipulate at their whim here on earth when disruptive or destructive thoughts enter our minds. Intrusive thoughts might even be a by-product from the energy of those who have already died here on earth. There is so little about the science of matter which is known, but I do know that there is always an exchange of energy taking place within our thoughts. Nothing is free, we are being translated by the spiritual thoughts of energy we take in towards glorified bodies in a realm called heaven or are seduced into remaining here on earth. We have the free will of a choice to choose our heritage of where we'll be planted at the end of our lives. So call upon a God who is now able to deliver you by our Lord and Savior and receive eternal life by the name of Jesus Christ because someone who lives eternally has the promises of what is true, Amen.

Stages of Birth in Eternal Life

In the beginning of creation, after all was set in order, God created man in His own image. "Male and female, created He them."

He blessed them with His presence and gave instruction: Be fertile and multiply. Fill the earth and subdue it.

He charged them over all the plants and animals except over the tree which bore the fruit of the knowledge of good and evil. It was pleasing to the eye with an aroma which smelt good. Yet, it was incomplete and rotten at its core with decay and death. For God warned that the day you eat of it you will surely die; take on its incomplete nature which lacked in the substance of His complete nature.

Adam, the first man, did not listen and the proof is that man stopped reflecting the truth of God's image. Adam now spoke from darkness rather than light and life, suffering the consequences of death. The presence of God went missing as he took on a nature of sin and now all men suffer a tainted blood-line which dies as it has been passed on through heredity to all men.

In addition, because we are severed from the vine of life, we die. We are now living like a withering branch cut off from the vine of life as we live to die within a tree of death. Our minds degenerate on the vine till becoming dim and making poor choices, we die quicker without any sight of the tree of life, which would allow us to live by the fruits of Him.

Presented with the problem of death, how does one reconnect to the vine of life with Adam's tainted blood while lacking the light of God's wisdom?

Good news, God being a creator has made a way where there was no way.

Psalm 8: Oh Lord, our Lord, how awesome is your name through all the earth our Lord! I will sing of Your majesty above the heavens with the mouths

of babes and infants. You have established the firmament against Your foes to silence the enemy who is
a darkened avenger. When I see Your heavens, the
work of Your fingers, the moon and stars that You
set in place, what is man that You are mindful of
Him and a son of man that You care for Him? Yet
You have made him a little less than a god, crowned
him with glory and honor. You have given him rule
over the works of your hand, put all things at his
feet: All sheep and oxen, even the beasts of the field,
the birds of the air, the fish of the sea, and whatever
swims the paths of the seas. Oh Lord, our Lord, how
awesome is Your name in all the earth.

A piece of God's essence enters by His Spirit
from heaven. At the same time, an egg drops to meet
with seed in the womb.

All is planned in the fertilization of fertility
within this threefold cord, a design not easily broken
in accordance with the choices any will make is
taking place. My earthen vessel shall die one day,
yielding to usher forth my living soul as seed to be
planted in heaven or hell by my choice to receive
God's promise or reject it.

Psalm 139: You formed me in my innermost being; you knit me in my mother's womb. I praise You, because I am wonderfully made; wonderful are Your works! My very self You know. My bones are not hidden from You, when I was being made in secret, fashioned in the depths of the earth. Your eyes saw me unformed; in your book all are written down; my days were shaped before one came to be. How precious to me are Your designs, oh God; how vast the sum of them! Were I to count them, they would outnumber the sands; when I complete them still You are with me.

Yes, I grow in the womb as the essence of my being is knit into a living soul by the Spirit of God's crafting hand. Next, I am planted to be formed in my mother's womb, and here, I experience growing into the fulness of its inner space until finding myself contained in a place of confinement. All have experienced going from one realm into another, sprouting forth at birth into life. Out I stretch from the darkness to enter into the light from out of my mother's earthen womb, having been fashioned into "being."

Yet the spirits of the wind blow, setting everything into motion and we soon forget "being." Now with nothing set in position, everyone turns to their own way and agrees that this is normal. Searching for a lost sight of the essence of God, which originally knit us together has been cut off. Silence forgotten and the quiet voice of "Truth" becomes dimmed, when in the dark of where the elements of God are hidden. Hid from sight till heart be pricked within a mind, which can only be shed by His light again. For losing our senses without the still moment of being rooted and grounded in the love of God, all sight of knowing Him has lost its luster altogether!

For our flesh rose up desiring release from the comfort of our blankets of swaddling when darkness called and into a tumbleweed pattern of existence we fell from freedom. The truth of love is not here to hold us in place. Now, prompted by spirits of the dark within the length of the breadth, passing through the heights and depths of time without restraints to quiet a living soul, we cannot be whole.

Once set in motion, all sight has become lost from our essence to have any meaning of "being."

Trying all things, there was no stillness to be found. We looked for light, but without God's presence all was gone while lost from sight as we searched to get back a full measure of light. Yes, we were removed from it to find no love in the dark.

There was no encounter with light to see the way to know Him anymore. We forgot being comforted while trying what the world had to offer, a drought could truly never quench our thirsts of dryness within our soul. Spirits of the discontent lay here, bringing dissatisfaction while confined inside our beings. All lacked the substance of earth as is in heaven and in my pride, even though weariness was heavily upon me, I was not ready to cry out. Then I realized that in my being, I was ready to die. Confined without answer to my problems without resolution, I twisted and turned in convulsion with no relief as the depth of my pain went unfathomed in the shallows. Still all remained dark as I drifted in a free fall without the comfort of a stable embrace while in my continual confinement of time and space. I became aware of the beast of a life which I could no longer bear to ride. Over I went into the dark, only I did not get up as I had no place to go. In surrender, my figuring mind came to a rest and in the stillness of helplessness, I found hope in a mercy of love that touched me from the inside out.

Ready for answers outside this world, I examined tears till finding no answer in a river run dry with desires of leaving my confinement of this world behind. I searched for a me that would answer me back. Fill my heart, until discovering the soundness of a return embrace that my foundation would no longer be shaken from place. The Lord offered me His hand at this very same time and I knew it was not mine. He opened my eyes to the light of His touch and I knew I wanted much more than mere existence! His love, more satisfying than my own sight, was so strong that I gave up my might while in the dark light. Knowing Him much more than this, I would find the me of purity entering in the letting go of my pride and confidence in myself ceased to exist as someone greater than the I of me was now here inside.

We search to find a life beyond our existence from without. Yet it is not until you look within and know that all is unmanageable in living a lie, you will not be ready for eternal life. For we are ready to take on a new nature when we allow God's word to move on the waters of our mind and refashion us back into the stillness of heaven. Then all becomes an experience of a full life by being reunited to God.

Now I am stilled from the commotions outside of "being." For I know I am in a world of no stability, all is in flux on shaky ground within its waves that I cannot see in my separation from stability. Have you crossed over, letting go of the spirits within your soul that could not satisfy a dying pride, which was killing all inside till crossing over in healing wings, soft and soothing to a soul, while embracing His Holy Spirit by God's full love?

Crafted to a redemptive fashion from the vine of death, anyone can be grafted to the vine of inner love. After a hatred of my creature self so intense, which brought misery inside my vision of the dark. I can now see to realize by God's light of love what was hidden. He crosses us over with His own pure blood, restoring by crafting touches of hand within our now quieted hearts through His justification of purity before God Almighty.

Yes! We chose His holy light to shine in life as justified darkness disappeared where instead of missing Him, now He is eternally near and even within. I will and have already been grafted into the Christ by a resurrection bloodline in the vine of life. It happened one line upon line of root at a time, woven into what is divine. One day I will be completely over there to receive my body glorified in full. For, I have received eternal life in the moment of forever called shalom.

Baptism

I had to learn that I was separated from God before I began to understand life. This is when wisdom started to come to light. At present, most of our understanding is dark. There is no reflection from God's Holy Spirit to have sight of what we truly look like when not clothed with His light. Now as shadows without the presence of brilliance to guide us, we are broken human beings from falling down in the dark. Born blind and naked, wretched and poor while incapable of being genuine in our love, we must allow God to first love us to know how to love ourselves before others. The real merciful crafting Character of Himself through the Holy Spirit truly teaches us how to have the boundaries to love all in life.

Originally, we were created to bear God's light, but the angel Lucifer (light bearer) fell into pride due to a jealousy of man. From the first, Adam was created to shine brighter and this enraged Lucifer. A rebellion was sparked of wanting to be even higher than God. Feeling slighted, the angel found itself cast out into time in outer darkness instead. He became Satan, the fallen god of a fallen world. Now while in a dim light, we cannot see that we are dying from being seduced into Satan's perversion of life. Truly in this devil's world, the darkness of death is disguised while what is real goes unnoticed and being alive becomes despised.

All men have been cut off from God's vine of life and grafted into a vine that produces death. For we are in an original heritage of rebellion by choice. Adam and Eve is of who I speak. The first man and woman created by God has made a choice for us all. Going against God's wise warning of not to partake of the fruit of the knowledge of good and evil was done. For God had warned, "The day you eat of it you will surely die."

So, here we are in a spiritual world of darkness as a puzzle in pieces (broken off) from the light of Christ's bloodline of life. Now seated in darkness without the reflection of God, we need His Holy Spirit to clothe us in His light. For He is the leader and guide into the fullness of truth to show us how to be put back together.

There are certain steps which need to take place for us to be reconnected to the Creator and living God. The first step is to hear how we have been broken away from the life that He gives and ask Him for His transformation. It is by the use of His crafting Hand that we are changed. The essence of death within the elements of a spiritual fallen world must be reconciled for us to be alive and experience His new life.

The second step is baptism that allows us to pass from being in the motion of darkness in a world of which dies till no longer trapped in Satan's world of time. When we admit we need to call upon God and acknowledge that a change has to happen to be moved from our brokenness, He grants eternal life. A call goes out for us to quiet ourselves and then we recognize His love among the wind which had raced our thoughts with anxiety. When the Holy Spirit enters, He leads us back to be connected to God by His own pure blood through resurrection while in the invited footsteps of a growing relationship with Christ.

God said, "Be still and know that I am God." Planting a seed in a hurricane is not possible. So, we need to learn how to slow down and enjoy Him in the moment throughout our busyness of day. Coming out from the commotions of time which divides to leave a darkness within a mind is essential. We have to learn how to call upon the Lord instead. For, "God is a rewarder of those who diligently seek the truth of the love He offers."

When coming out of our way of doing things, the first thing we discover is friction from going against our usual routine. You will hear from others, "How come you are not like you used to be?" or "Why did you stop spending time with us?"

Next comes heat as you start to feel discomfort from within. Thoughts as voices will enter your mind and tell you to go back to what the world has to offer.

Spirits shall try to convince you that comforts are a necessity to distract from receiving the full measure of God's love. When you hear, "Look at what God blesses with," do not get distracted from the giver of the blessings as I've come to know that I want only Him. For only God can satisfy all your needs with the abundance of a full life. His words of truth shall lead to a full relationship of love with His regenerative "Blood" by resurrection, contained within a bloodline of life, which prepares all to go through what will come next. Voices that burn with the fire of lies shall say, "Go back, it is much too difficult. People are going to think you're crazy and then no one will want to be around you." Though when God is your Lord and friend, you can tell when someone is loving towards you. So, follow His instructions like in the days of Noah who listened to Him. God told him to prepare an ark to save him, his family, and all the animals, and he did as He asked. When you trust someone is true, you never walk alone. For it takes one man and one God to make a majority to push back the spiritual forces of this world. Deliverance awaits, as The Messiah is the second ark of God's plan. Get on board, receive eternal life and you shall tread on the heads of scorpion-demons and serpents. For when a compulsive entity tries to block you from His light of life, remember, "Greater is He that is in me than he that is in this world."

After fire, there is light and entering all the way through this door of friction, heat, till burning with fire into light, you will pass from the darkness of all that is dim and ignite into eternity by asking to remain with Him. For through the new flesh and blood covenant of Jesus Christ, His resurrection seed enters inside to co-mingle within each new renewal of eternal life.

Completion is known when His cycle reconnects to regenerate you alive until fully glorified. Jesus said, "I am the light and the life of all men" and "I am the way, the truth and the life. No man comes to the Father of creation, but by me."

Baptism prepares us by being buried with The Christ through the nature of His word, which originally moved upon the waters. He raises us up with the craft of His hand to become a part of His church. Preparation has now occurred to be married to Him as His living Bride. For unlike being planted in destruction by Satan's deception that has imprisoned men in this realm of time, we are set free to be born anew. The bodies that house our living souls are being put to death. For once we were captured and bound to this world, but through water baptism, we can be planted in eternity instead.

When all is set in place, a reception of eternal life happens through the seed of resurrection. We have been prepared to receive our bridegroom and Christ. Prepared for what God promises in the way of new glorified bodies, which will house and contain eternal living souls much more than what any spirits can offer us here on earth. We are reconnected to God by His Holy Spirit while on this planet and at the same time deposited in heaven. Growing to receive our new eternal life tents to physically match beyond the gates of pearl. God's heart must be searched for with a full intensity to reach it. I had to tear it out of His chest and place it within my own. He, the great physician, supervises by the mercy of His own blood of love. For when both of our hearts beat together as one and the same within my chest, I truly know I have a relationship with Him.

At baptism, the Holy Spirit enters and guides us by grace, adorning all into what compliments complete holiness. Caught up into the heights of purity by His glorifying light, we are directed into a deeper heartfelt love than ever before. For after passing through the valley of the shadow of death by God's authority, the Messiah unites us with His living blood.

Continue to ask Jesus Christ to work the essence of His resurrecting power in you and His righteous changes will take effect. For when God does the work, He proves Himself true. Now what is at rest upon our heads is the crown of life, which is a lighter burden than the pressures of this world. For when having a sincere faith, a clear conscience, and a pure heart, we know that the taste of death has been removed. We're now kept alive by the taste of His living blood, sweeter than honeycomb.

Jesus said, "Unless you are born again you shall not inherit the Kingdom of God."

You may ask yourselves, "How can I be born again? Shall I enter my mother's womb a second time?"

Jesus further says, "No one can enter the Kingdom of God without being born of water and spirit. What is born of flesh is flesh and what is born of spirit is spirit."

I know my flesh is dying by my own mortality. So, my attention was drawn to look at the properties of what happens to water within its cycle because everything in life has cycles. As all of creation: Animals, birds, insects, plants and men all operate in cycles. Even the earth has cycles as in every 7th year of jubilee, one seventh of the land has to be rested. Man on every seventh day - called a sabbath day - enters back into being in the moment with God to be reminded of the enjoyment of His "rest" of presence, "Shabbat Shalom." God carries us throughout the physical labors of the week while resting in Him as we enter though the door of, Shalom. Yet to fully understand the Messiah is to acknowledge our broken spiritual connection from God.

After first recognizing all of the other cycles, I could tell that something was missing between me and my Maker. It was a cycle that if remained unfixed, I would continue to walk in the confusion of the dark. We all walk blindly without any true light of sight or having a full essence of intimacy in relations with Him. For while under the deception of knowing God darkly, in name only, there is no true connection to Him.

When baptized, we enter into the oneness of water, which evaporates up into the acquiescence of our firmament. We become replenished by each new cycle upon meeting with the water as rain when it collects as vapor to return to replenish our earth, it is a type of rebirth. I believe it is to become one with the law of all nature, which God has established as a testimony. All of creation testifies through His word, which originally moved upon the waters at the dawn of all creation. For God has said, "All of creation testifies of Himself."

I also took a look at the nature of the Holy Spirit which crafts us back into eternal life with the use of the Sacrificial Lamb that repairs our connection to

God. Jesus Christ's regenerative resurrection living blood replaces Adam's degenerative bloodline of death. Yes, at the marriage supper of the lambs table of the Holy Eucharist, we are co-mingled with eternal life. Re-aligning us line upon line, precept upon precept one root at a time. Here a little there a little for a greater clarity of God's character allows us to better understand how to focus on the face of Christ completely.

We are redeemed from the spirits of this world that held us to the law of a broken spiritual connection, which kept us from receiving a full life with God. For Adam's sin caused us all to enter being grafted into a death that we needed to be redeemed back from. We went missing from being complete and without light, there was no finding our God in the dark. Now we are joined to eternal life where the cycle of the living bloodline joins us to God's redemption. We have been reconnected for us to go to our new heavenly bodies by the truth of God's reconciliatory love.

Baptism prepares us to receive our bridegroom, Jesus Christ, where joined in unity and aligned with a new spiritual nature, we are woven into his body, the gathering, which we know as the church. Now, we as bride can receive our bridegroom's resurrection seed found in the flesh and blood of the Holy Eucharist. We are now sealed though the Holy Spirit's reconnection to the cycle of light where resurrection through the blood of Christ begins instantly as all who believe are ushered back up into the perpetual eternity of life. For being seated in heavenly heights with Jesus Himself, all through the crafting of the Holy Spirit, we are on the way to being completely reconnected from the broken spiritual truth that was missing from life. Now being grafted, our roots are grounded into and by the love of Christ.

Picture God's cycle as a lightning connection with a bolt that connects us with light. Adam broke the connection between us and God which turned out the light of the Holy Spirit by severing us from The tree of Life. The Son Of God's regenerative blood restores when choosing His plan for life. For if we otherwise partake of His Eucharist meal in an unworthy manner, we would be sealed to remain in a broken state and encounter an eternal death in life's place.

Now pressing through all of darkness, we have been seated in heavenly places with the Christ. As it is written, "If you search for me with all your heart, you will find me." Now at the altar of the marriage supper of the lamb's table, the light has come on and darkness put out, for we have been joined by the new covenant blood of Jesus that refashions a man to make him whole. This is done by the Holy Spirit guiding us into a fullness of light after water baptism.

In baptism when we are born again, where do we go? The scriptures say, "We are in this world, but no longer of it." We have now been joined to eternal life while here in time. I say again, "The light has come on by the living blood of Jesus Christ. We have been regenerated by eternal life. For as the Holy Spirit provides direction for regenerative blood to flow through us, again through being baptized, His light aluminates us with sight by resurrection life. Now dead and buried beneath the water through baptism, having been prepared to become one with Christ, all has been set in order. We are raised back up from the spiritual darkness of this world to receive the stages which grow us into eternal life in the now to walk with Him on earth.

When does the work of this cycle of being introduced to eternal life end? When we get our new physical bodies we break ties with this world and gain heaven beyond our heritage of old degenerative flesh. We are no longer a puzzle in pieces, for we know what we will look like by God's guiding light, "For though we now look through a mirror darkly, one day we shall know Him as He is, for we shall see Him face to face." We have been finally pieced back together by the mercy of God's grace.

God has a plan. We either get planted here on earth by rejecting it through living rebellious lives or slowly move out of our bodies by growing out of them while under the guidance of the Holy Spirit. All it takes is being willing to ask God to change you in each stage of growth when prompted to do so.

Truth allows us to be completely grafted into the vine of life (one root of transfer at a time in each area of our lives).

Herein we draw from the sap of Christ's living blood, available to grant us access into heaven by being grafted back into Him. We are changed by being wrapped in God's threads of truth by His word, pointing to the New Covenant, which now translates us through a kind of metamorphosis.

A caterpillar turning into a butterfly is our example of a law found in nature which testifies of the handiwork of God. For we are able to fly from our bodies spiritually and enter back into eternity or become trapped in our cocoons of earthen vessels to become harvested by demon powers as a degenerated eternal living soul of energy.

A perpetual painful death lay waiting for all who are prideful enough to do things their own way. There will be no escaping as souls shall continually die to a weeping and wailing and gnashing of teeth without getting needs met. For they have been deceptively led to suffer the fate of having unfulfilled desires. Harvested without any rest where a perpetually release of energy happens while in a non satisfying tormented eternal condition.

Foul Spirits deceive by driving all into the reach of a motion for something not obtainable and while under this delusional illusion, any who remain in the dark will be used and abused at the whim of these dragons while being continually drained.

Baptism opens the door to be reconnected to God by the resurrection bloodline of Christ to comprehend pure light with sight and understand eternity with life. Now I suggest that you follow God's plan and be baptized in the name of the Father, Son, and Holy Ghost and secure His promises by becoming a part of the body of Christ; where once sealed in holiness, you shall have a joyous eternal life.

We All Speak from a Pulpit

We all give proclamations from pulpits that we stand before while on the move in life. The choices behind our actions and words while interacting with others yields energy from our living souls towards a power for creation that leads to life or death situations which concern us all. This is why, "We are to take every thought captive under the subjection of Jesus Christ."

For when we practice something we do not fully understand, we walk comprehending a skewed reality that oppressively abuses us in the dark. We encounter societal abuse and practice deeming it normal rather than fellowshipping with the light of love as we fall away from the protection of God.

For when we lack understanding in acknowledging God's wisdom, the truth is not in us and we practice partaking in a reality with deceptive spirits behind a veil of lies instead. We are born into a dark world where the truth is not in us. For without any light to see, there are only spirits that exist inside our living soul which have taken us captive. Their purpose is to lie to keep us in darkness, steal our life force of energy, and keep reality smashed so that we can perpetually be destroyed. They want to feed from our eternal life source of continual energy from our living souls inside our earthen vessels of flesh to keep us permanently in their hellish domain.

The issues of life and death are in the tongue as according to scripture, "We will be held accountable for every dot and tittle out of place" that we create by verdicts of judgment without discernment where we wound the conscience of others and ourselves in the process. Thank God for the grace of His mercies that are new every morning that allow us to be reconciled with Him from moment to moment and day by day. For Jesus said, "Forgive them Father for they know not what they do," allowing a grace for us to walk in holiness by His cleansing through regenerative transforming blood. Let us be grateful that He chose to die on the cross out of merciful love for us all, as He has brought eternal life.

Now, "We are to be alert and wakefully watchful with all diligence as the devil is a roving lion seeking whom he may devour." This means we must watch what we say according to God's word so as to not place ourselves in Hell by our own actions of judgment. For if we are not looking at love and truth in balance when we talk with others, we are out of harmony with the God of light and place ourselves back in darkness to be used and abused by the minion spirits of this world.

Keep in mind that for every action, there is an equal and opposite reaction. Nothing is for free as there is an interactive exchange of energy always taking place between individuals that can either divide or bring people closer together in exchanging ideas. For it is not just what we say but how it is being said. So, do not speak in anger or you will blind yourself through your own bad attitudes, habits, or hangups that shall block you from having peace to express yourself in a full and loving joyous way as might for right leaves everyone here. For when not drunk with other spirits, we are filled with the Holy Spirit, which brings gladness to resist the devil that we may flee from all appearances of evil as God's love restrains and allows us to slip through the enticements of the devil.

Reasoning the weight of truth together should create a deeper mutual respect for one another as the deep calls unto the deep together. "For as iron sharpens iron so does the countenance of a good friend," which allows one the dignity of a mutual respect when examining disputes to move from darkness to revelations of enlightenment. For when everything is more deeply understood it allows for the most satisfying meal of all as only pure truth will displace and dismember all falsehoods.

Remember, "When the blind lead the blind the two fall into a ditch," and get hurt as "The simple pass on and get punished." Might does not make right, reason does, as it allows for personal growth in place of the destruction of war.

So, kick the elephant in the room off your pulpits that you can see to replace any lie within darkness with light and in the process discover deliverance by the real Jesus Christ.

A World Within A World

"For God so loved the world that He gave His only begotten Son that whosoever believes in Him might not perish but have eternal life. For God did not send His Son in the world to condemn the world, but that the world may be saved through Him. Whoever believes in Him will not be condemned, but whoever does not believe has already been condemned because he has not believed in the name of the only Son of God."

The question has recently come to mind, which world was God referring to that did not become condemned? The earth consists of everything that has been established by the blood of the lamb's regenerative resurrected elements. In the beginning, He was slain from before the foundation of the world that our world, having seen creation through a bloodline of life could exist. Consisting of 3/4 water and 1/4 of land, along with vegetation, animals with mobility, and what teamed with life in the sea under a great dome, our world has a self-sustaining system that keeps replenishing itself.

Our systems also contain reproduction, electrical impulses, lungs shaped like trees that produce oxygen, wind and storms, digestion, acid pools, light, contributories that return to the sea, earthquakes, sound waves, volcanic eruptions from gasses which creates new earth matter, and all other elements that replenish themselves through cycles in a contained environment. As when a limb is cut, it forms bark like scabs from the oozing of its sap like blood. Mankind was created from this world, formed from the earth as a smaller world crown of creation glory to form a contained world with a world of his own.

We are a peculiar people, fearfully and wonderfully made. Created creatures having a living soul of energy in an earthen vessel set up within a world of flesh within a dome of our own. With lungs that breathe the breath of life, our sneezes a storm, and a brain with electrical impulses with thoughts that strike like lightning as they connect with emotions to produce cognitive feelings. Our digestive tracts work like vegetation which produce acid and our bowels erupt like volcanoes with gas and all else. Then like trees which lose their leaves in seasons our hair turns gray and as we age we suffer, too. No more to brush as it has fallen, balding till all is left bald barren upon the ground. Like leaves, our hair is everywhere, a foreshadowing until we will one day topple.

We are 3/4 blood and water, 1/4 land with tributaries as rivers and have mobility like animals. Yes, there is a lot going on in our reproductive gardens along with all else. As when there is light with understanding, we are walking by the truth of God's love hand in hand. However, when there's light without understanding, we are led to believe we are walking alone while continuing on in Adam's heritage of a degenerative blood which dies. Due to his rebellious nature of pride, now we all have to experience death. We walk in the breadth here within the heights and depths of the length of the framework of time where until we humble ourselves, there is no experiencing God's world of eternal life. Choices have been made for us to walk under the cloak of the prince of darkness, which were never intended for us instead.

Our living souls were originally given to us to walk in the light of fellowship with God's love like a closed lightning circle to experience a perpetual exchange of it. "We love because He first loved us," allowing for full feelings in an abundance of life.

Now on a larger level, our world orbits in cycles around the sun in a solar system that orbits within the Milky Way and they in turn orbit around other galaxies, which orbit within a universe that perhaps folds over on itself and giving an appearance of infinity.

"Walk in the light while you have the light so that darkness does not overtake you."

Before the fall of man, he was created in God's image and shone clothed in glory light. In a perpetual edification of the Holy Spirit, the stability of an unshakeable sound mind was his along with a regenerative bloodline that never knew corruption. Man was God's offspring and as the fruit doesn't fall far from the tree, I believe he was to be trained in the art of creation. Man knew not the gift he had and before it could be realized, there was something else in the garden which contained no harmony with balance and knew how to kill while aware of this, too.

Lucifer (light bearer) became Satan, wanting the energy of living souls to suit his purposes rather than God's. So within Adam's nature, the fallen angel led his helpmate, Eve, the weaker vessel to be seduced away from trusting in God's voice first.

In marriage, two are joined to become one flesh as Adam had said, "Bone of my bone, flesh of my flesh." Upon seeing Eve, as God had crafted her from his rib. Eve, being a part of Adam, took His eyes off God and chose to become a part of the nature of an evil he knew existed in death. Here he took his eyes from looking at the light of God, which had him clothed in a Holiness of Spirit, and looked into the darkness of her sin and took on a cloak of darkness of his own as he entered in. Man became grafted into a tree of death while he followed Eve into sin and God went missing when he broke his connection with Him.

Adam then lost his bloodline of life while breaking connection with His light, but not the gift of His living soul.

Now that Satan had them out of the garden, this fallen angel waited patiently to have the energy of Adam's living soul for his own and all his offspring. For this fallen angel knew that if he could keep man walking in darkness, there would be no reconnecting with God's hand of love by the light and life of all men.

Satan's main weapon is darkness unto this day. For in darkness there is a confusion where mankind is caused to practice what is not understood till losing sight of all truth in a web of lies. For while cut off from light and missing God, he can forget His attributes that are kind, gentle, and patient in an act of love within all His character. For the devil knows if he can convince mankind that Jesus is a God of condemnation and not conviction with forgiveness, mercy, and compassion, no one will then want to go to Him.

In a world of darkness, there are minion spirits that we do not see. These dragons try to get us to act out by offering us dead things in exchange for our living energy that comes from our souls. For energy is never used up. It is either transferred or stored and for every action there is an equal and opposite reaction.

When we pick up things to abuse our body, in essence kill ourselves by living with addictive tendencies that rob us of what it is to truly be alive, we allow minions entrance into our soul to devour us and create pain in place of love. Though once becoming grafted into the vine of light from out of the dark, our minds get sharpened as thoughts connect with emotions. Then comes a fuller, feeling, and brilliant life with sight. Trying to get satisfaction in an unsatisfying world then becomes a thing of the past, for having eternal life in this world, we no longer have part with the minions that are of it. Now freed from being connected to the spirits bound to time, we have reconnected to the Holy Spirit in eternity and here in lie satisfaction.

We had allowed Satan to plunder us by walking hand and hand with Him instead of God, only we did not see it before. For our light of focus from thoughts and emotions being torn from the abusive life styles surrounding us has made our mind dim.

We were in the midst of walking in darkness on shaky ground within unstable waves of time that we could not see from over the top of the dunes of shifting sands in order to find the rock of Christ to stand on. Energy from a living soul was being stolen here. We would have been bound perpetually to weeping and wailing without being heard as minions gnashed their teeth, if not for Jesus Christ who was, and is, and is yet to come. For in the choice of His obedience as the second Adam unto death mankind lacks nothing as God is fair. The end result of his choice, Jesus reconciles us to God to ignite our souls, again to be used for God's purpose. The rewards are great while in service to Him as He is eternal life and light.

For when the New Testament points to the New Covenant during this process, everything brilliantly shines through the mind of Christ where all falls back into place. The regenerative resurrection blood renews and restores our relationship with God. It is reconnecting us all in an electrically charged Holy Spirit cycle of light, as John the Baptist said, "I am the voice of the one who cries out in the desert. Make straight the way of the Lord. I baptize with water but there is one of you who you do not recognize." (For man could not see out from over the crests of spiritual forces where darkness drives the winds in our fallen state where our minds are blocked from seeing any glimpse of light.)

Now stilled by the Holy Spirit, we are no longer driven. We have been prepared by going through the door from darkness unto light instead. For now joined to the living bloodline of His Holy Eucharistic flesh and blood thanksgiving meal, we experience the seed of Jesus Christ. He enters into us "His Bride" at every marriage supper of the lamb's New Covenant gathering. Both the new testament along with the laws found in the cycles of nature testify of this. The devil tries to conceal this fact very well by twisting scriptures that the word of truth is not rightly divided in the Bible. Yet when the truth is known to point to the resurrection, eternal life is clearly found in the new covenant. It is essential to read with understanding or after one dies there will be no resurrection. Yet for those who persevere, faith allows them to continue to receive resurrection while here on earth while having their eternal glorified body prepared in heaven as a part of closing the broken cycle that joins us on earth as it is in heaven.

No longer is energy transferred into being stolen by weeping and wailing and gnashing of teeth anymore. For the joy of the Lord has become our strength from receiving heaven perpetually. God again walks with us in His garden even while on earth as we shall keep receiving eternal life from Him now and forever, Amen.

Lost & Found

Jesus said, "If you lose your life for my name's sake, you will find it." "…that I may know Him and the power of His resurrection, and the fellowship of His sufferings, being conformed to His death, if, by any means, I may attain to the resurrection from the dead."

In making room for God in my life, I am learning the art of dying to myself in many different stages to allow light to shine in my darkness and bring life by way of the cross of Christ.

My desire to get ahead in this world's system has turned from working to accumulate things for myself to supporting my wife and children. Then came the art of serving God with my talents in place of serving myself. A talent is something that God gifts you to enjoy doing in life. Something that comes easy till you discover its futility in that being number one is a lonely place when you're by yourself. I knew I needed something more for me to use my craft of writing as it served me no purpose. It was boring writing for myself. I put down my pen and refused to pick it up again as I had no reason to.

So, I worked odd jobs to be in the company of others till I discovered that they were just as lonely as me. How dark and depressing life had become and though I searched to find out while trying the any of everything, there was no answer to why?

Then came God who answered my question and this gave me reason in life to be alive. I now had purpose. I could tell others that they did not have to be lonely anymore because there is a living God who loves them and would always care for and protect them as we are all His creations. We are children with a special design with a specific purpose in mind that He has given each one of us.

Now I had a reason to write, which gave me purpose for living. My pen became a fountain of life when I held it before God's light to answer the question of how others could find Him, too. Now, there would be no more darkness, just as long as I would use my pen in hand while in service to Him. No matter what, I shall follow Him with my talent of pen as I Know that life has a meaning which will always be fresh when using my craft of writing in service to Him. I have found a life that became a precious gift, "My burden is easy and My yoke is light" when it comes from Christ. For it is always fresh and without weight, which makes its rewards great, during this shift of life here on earth with my pen. Best of all, the Creator of everything had become my intimate friend. I now know that I will never be lonely or alone again.

The body craves a perversion of pleasure called lust and once hooked by this inroad of spiritual darkness, it makes it even harder to find what satisfies. The light of the love which comes from God would never allow us to abuse ourselves in the name of love. It is a masterful work of the devil to try to get our needs met through loving material things and of flesh which can never satisfy us eternally, but perpetuate an existence of confusion and pain instead. For who knows how to love us better spiritually beyond the maze of a labyrinth of false religions than the God who has created us?

God's heart aches over us because everyone has seemingly turned unto their own way to make themselves comfortable in a world of dark illusions. They really do not see that they are being led down a path by the forces of spirits which blind them for their own personal gain. Yes, there are spirits which seek our demise for destruction so they can continue to feed off of our living souls like cattle being led to the slaughter. Only these dragons feed off of us with teeth so fine that we do not recognize with each hit of emotional pain that there are forces at work which perpetually draw our energy from us. Every time we reach towards an addictive seduction with dissatisfaction, they get a meal. Not only do they feed off us now, but for all eternity they will feed, if we are not awakened out of darkness to enter into the light of Christ for them to be burned off us and scurry away by the heat of God's intensity of love. Be cautious or they perhaps will possess your life giving and living soul of energy throughout an everlasting eternity.

For when we are blind to the spiritual forces that surround us, this is what I call being lost.

Finding out what I just shared is the first step to being fully found by God's love. For How can anyone ask our Great Physician to heal us if we first do not know the complete symptoms of what is ailing us? See the problem of what ails us first and then you can ask God to heal your hearts and minds to fully embrace what He is offering in the way of eternal life.

Lord, I see my problems by the light and life of Your Son. He is revealing all to me by the power of His flesh and blood, which has entered into me through the co-mingling of Your Eucharistic thanksgiving meal. For now at the marriage supper of the lamb's table, I ask that You purify me to receive the full measure of preparation of what you have in store for me. I no longer desire to be lost but completely possessed by the guidance of Your Holy Spirit. So make me whole by the timing of Your wisdom so that I may be found forever. Save us from the futility of our carnal and fleshly minds that You may have authority over everything foul that hides in the dark which draws energy from our life. Place Your mind within me so I may always breathe the breath of heaven, which can only be found by wearing Your crown of life. Thank You for loving me enough to die for me, the way You did at Golgotha on that grueling cross of agony with each drop of blood. You have made me beyond happy as a joyful sheep in Your pasture where under Your protection, soundness has recaptured my mind. My Great Shepherd, You are the restorer of my soul. Amen.

Now I seek to read the scriptures in a way that their eternal truth can rightly be divided.

The New Covenant has my focus and I draw from the flesh and blood root of Him while looking through portions of verse. Otherwise, I cannot receive the correct eternal picture of what they have to offer, "For the demons know the scriptures, too, and they tremble." Twisting the scriptures is Satan's last defense at keeping us his prisoners and this taskmaster does not treat his slaves kindly. For I, myself, became liberated when I stopped wrestling the scriptures to my own destruction while compulsively being driven to share a false gospel without peace.

God's kingdom is a kingdom of peace and so shall his message be preached in like fashion. Jesus, being the king of peace, should not leave you feeling anxious but leave you having a deeper faith and trust in Him.

For His ability to change the essence of your being can only happen when asked while all is being revealed to you. Where He is missing in your life should not be left up to you for salvation, for we need an incorruptible God to save us from our corruption of blood. It must be realized that you cannot do this by yourself when brought to light.

When something is brought to light where you are missing God's presence in your life, there is a necessity for it to be resolved by His gift of eternal life. He must be in you or a deception will lead you to believe that you are complete when you are not. He lives in you when His weight right now outweighs what the world has to offer by loving Him more in return. God wants to deliver us all from the minion spirits that are in this world. Yet, due to our pride with our own feeble attempts at trying to serve Him in His standard of Holiness, we remain in the flesh and miss taking His hand.

James 4:3-8, "You do not possess because you do not ask. You ask but do not receive because you ask wrongfully to spend it on your passions. Adulterers! Do you not know to be lovers of the world is to be at enmity with God? Therefore, whoever wants to be a lover of this world makes himself an enemy of God. Or do you suppose that the scripture speaks without meaning when it says, "The Spirit that He has made to dwell in us tends towards jealousy?" But He bestows a greater grace; therefore, it is written, "God resists the proud, but gives grace to the humble."

So, submit yourself to God. Stand still and firm and remember Him as your first love in the heat of when being tempted by the devil (do not forget the truth of love's embrace) and in the greater light this fallen angel's cloak of darkness will dissipate. Be left embraced and protected by the truth of His love alone. Learn to fully wait on Him and deliverance will come. Draw near to God and He will draw near to you." For as you wait on Him in the heat of any battle, He shall deliver you.

In a true rest from the burdens of anything you are facing, they will fall away. So, move into the deeper trust of, "God is able to bring to completion that good work which He has started in you." You will then enjoy the presence of His company over anything else that comes your way while in service to Him. For, "He is the vine and we are the branches and apart from Him we can do nothing." So, when having a plan or an agenda of our own, we dry out and whither pretty quickly when not being in line with His vine. Do not cut yourselves off by going off on your own. Trying to get a dark choice to fit in with God's light is a wrong direction.

Finding ourselves outside of a vision of The Christ, we become swamped by our own waves of divisiveness which becomes a distraction from God. When faith becomes shipwrecked, you must remember to set your eyes back on Jesus as a drowning man needs to yield in order to be rescued.

The direction of God grows us back into place to leave us at peace on the safety of His rock. We are not to take matters into our own hands and say that it is the Lord's burden by going some place on our own either. For when life becomes dry, other spirits shall meet with your hands to misdirect you on a path of destruction, but it is to suit God's purposes of getting your attention. For, "The Lord chastens whom He loves."

These are some eternal life lessons on how the Lord has operated in my life, which helps me to discern whether or not I am heading in the right or wrong direction. For even when hardships come, if I can still enjoy God's presence and intimacy in the midst of them, I know I am found in the place of where He would have me to be.

After 46 years of walking with my Lord Jesus Christ, I learned that it is good to know God with understanding. "Study to show yourselves approved." Having light and not confusion establishes a foundation of peace for me to see where I am going. His intimate love builds up to contain a full life. Joy flows throughout the marrow of my bones and into a fountain of strength as I have discovered eternal life. So, do not build reality on the sinking sands of time but on the rock of eternity instead and you will be forever blessed.

When you are genuine, you will be able to love others as yourself while feeding from the same trough before God. This is a fountain which establishes you on earth as it is in heaven, for you are feeding from the real "Tree of Life."

I Don't Wanna Die!

A

One Act

Play

By

R. A. Feller

I Don't Wanna Die!

Dark room - spotlight fades in on a man sitting on a stool dressed in black.

Man: I don't wanna die!

Voice from Dark: You will one day, same as anybody else.

Man: But I've worked so hard to have everything I have…

Voice from Dark: Might as well get used to it.

Man: Who said that?

SILENCE: (3 seconds)

Voice from Dark: Just must be a thought.

Man: Wait! Am I here for a reason? A purpose I've not considered?

Voice from Dark: Same as anybody else?

Man: Never considered death before. So many voices have had me distracted since youth.

SILENCE: (3 Seconds)

Man: My life? Is there anything I could have missed? Hmmm! Wrapped in a blanket as babe, restricted. Now, here I stand confined having tried it all… and yet, I still cannot move, constricted! There must be a more? Or maybe a before?

Voice from Dark: You're imagining things.

Man: How did I get here in this place so dark, which hurts my emotions from a lack of understanding me.

Voice from Dark: Ask a relative?

Man: No, it's irrelevant!

Voice from Dark: I said, "A relative."

Another spot fades in on a white-faced angel sitting across from him on another stool.

Man: (looks over with a gasp) Who are you?

Angel: I have been sent by God.

Man: Why are you here?

Angel: Because you've questioned death.

Man: How come I could not see you before?

Angel: Because your mind was dim within the test
of time while moving through the breadth until
a prayer of another beamed a thought of light to
see death. It is a mercy inside your mind.

Man: Then if God is real, the story I heard about
Adam and Eve is true, too.

Angel: Everything was made from the blood of life
which sang with harmony in the beginning
when Lucifer shined so bright.

Man: Then there is a devil, too.

Angel: Yes, Lucifer shined brightly till Man shined
brighter. It split Satan's mind into a jealous
fallen double. An eternal living soul, clothed
by earthen vessel, in the Holy Spirit light kept
away this creature of night.

Man: What are you saying?

Angel: High crowned creation, masterpiece of God, above the music of this angelic creature… It was just too much for one made so proud to bear.

Man: But I have no vision to see what you say on my own unless by your' sight you grant me more light.

Angel: A war ensued, making Lucifer dark. Scratched by anger, man became an adversary to hate as Satan hated all till cast out in realm of time, separated from eternity and the harmony of God.

Man: How can this be?

Angel: You questioned death. Do you want to know more?

Voice from Dark: It's a waste of time.

Man: This is a waste of time:

Angel: You cannot see, but you can hear. For the thought that's in your mind was the devil's not your own as by Satan's cloak of darkness, confusion is man's home.

Man: So, you say that confusion is darkness then?

Angel: Can you get very far without being dissatisfied?

Man: Why, no.

Angel: Everything happens in cycles of nature. Water rains down and returns by its atmosphere to the earth as seed bearing plants. Animals return as well. Yet man, God's crown, contains all created within where the Spirit clothed him in light until broken.

Man: I see that I've been grafted from tree of life to darkest death while hidden under Satan's cloak.

Angel: Slow down and you'll discover all discomfort comes from looking at their deceptive sights. "Where are you going?" is a dark voice with fright. While God speaks, "Be still and know My light."

Man: You're making me feel uncomfortable.

Angel: Beyond the discomforts of heat, burning fire, till there is an entrance by His door of light, know that forces will be pushed back to reveal what happens to a living soul when an earthen vessel dies at night.

Man: Then The Christ has come to flow through me by a regenerative blood and baptism. They must connect my bonds to flow in eternal life by resurrection.

Angel: You're pretty quick to catch the vision of this light.

Man: It's by His word (points up) my messenger
that I have light to walk with sight. For understanding has brought me joy to now have
strength within my life.

Angel: Yes, He is the light and the life of all men and
so much more.

Man: What do you mean by so much more?

Angel: What is the purpose of the resurrection?

Man: To one day receive eternal life.

Angel: No, the resurrection is now and a part of an
eternity of life. For in this world and no longer
of it, there is no strife when you're in heaven
with Christ.

Man: How could this be possible?

Angel: Consider the metamorphosis of a butterfly,
for every law in nature testifies of God.

SILENCE: (2 Seconds)

Man: I'm listening.

Angel: A caterpillar wrapping itself in threads of truth, forming a cocoon in nature, is an example of what happens spiritually as a part of God's handiwork. You fly as a living soul, shedding from your body to enter eternity and receive a glorified reward.

Man: What happens if we do not escape our vessels as I've seen many butterflies not leave their cocoons?

Angel: There will be weeping, wailing, and gnashing of fine razor minion teeth. You feel the pain behind your emotional bruises, do you not?

Man: Yes.

Angel: Unfulfilled desires cause duress as energy is never depleted but transferred or stored. For every stress pressing in and not turned over to God, releases energy in pride that demons feed upon.

Man: Collated files of thought inside mind I have relied on were never mine. I see. I've been fed actions not my own. Reacting since youth where robbed of my life, I only had darkness presumed to be light, which has distracted me from preparing a proper cocoon. For I die inside when not able to spread wings to fly.

Angel: A perpetual painful death lay waiting for the proud who do not listen. No escaping the weep and wail, gnashing of teeth where desires are not met and frustrations feed all savage energy draining beasts.

Man: What a deception to suffer dark torn feelings where dragons feeding pull us apart as they lay more eggs between mind and heart.

Angel: They harvest every unhatched soul, leaving none to rest, tormenting demons continue to do this best. Foul spirits drive all to reach for illusions to use and abuse an eternal living soul at whim.

Man: My soul shall sail with wings and glide unto heaven.

Angel: Just as one vine caused death to enter in by the fruit of a knowledge of good and evil, through realm of paradise unto fallen earth, another vine as "The Tree of Life" is here as well in a parallel to intersect all back, translated to God's kingdom. The man stretches and yawns saying, "What a comforting thought," then dozes off to sleep.

Angel: No, don't go to sleep!

The man starts to snore for a few moments on the stool, but then quickly awakes and stretches…

Man: Must have been a dream.

The man gets up and leaves the spotlight on an empty stool.

SILENCE: 4 seconds

Voice from darkness: Laughs sinisterly. [As the spotlight fades to black.]

When the lights come on, a giant prop serpent is seen on stage.

Serpent: (Same as voice from the dark) You're all doomed!

Angel: (Still sitting on stool) Liar!

The serpent slinks along off stage exiting as the angel looks up towards heaven. The curtain comes down.

- The End -

Other Books

"The Playground"

Calingtoncastle.com
"Calington Castle Series"

"Love Notes for my Butterfly"

"Poems & Scraps for Healing and Growth"

www.ingramcontent.com/pod-product-compliance
Lightning Source LLC
Chambersburg PA
CBHW051852130726
47987CB00002B/797